The Weather Dress

a story by Catherine Fisher

illustrated by Maggie Davies

PONT

To Marjorie Coopey

In memory of Pete Bailey

Published in Wales in 2006 by Pont Books, an imprint of
Gomer Press, Llandysul, Ceredigion, SA44 4JL

ISBN 1 84323 593 5
ISBN-13 9781843235934

A CIP record for this title is available from the British Library.

This book is published with the financial support of the
Welsh Books Council

Printed and bound in Wales at
Gomer Press, Llandysul, Ceredigion SA44 4JL
www.gomer.co.uk

Halfway through Chepstow market, Molly saw the stall. On the counter was a jumble of clothes and interesting toys.

She dumped her bag. 'Hello.'

'Hello,' the thin man said. 'Call me Sol.' He sat on a high stool, among hanging suns, old teddies, skipping ropes and glitters of beads.

Sol's eyes were sharp and sky blue. He spread his long fingers out. 'Let me grant you a wish. What would you like most?'

Molly thought. 'I'd like to go to the seaside. But it's always raining.'

Sol smiled. 'How much money have you got?'

olly stepped closer. There were wooden boxes, and a doll with odd-coloured eyes. She touched a tin monkey, and it turned and winked at her. 'Only a pound.'

'That may be enough. Try there.' He pointed to a pile of clothes.

Molly's hand went into the pile; she felt something smooth and rich as velvet and she pulled it out. It was a dress.

The dress was old, with a tear in the hem. It seemed to be a mix of colours, like a watery rainbow.

'That's a Weather Dress,' Sol said. 'It will last you six days, but you mustn't wear it for seven. The seventh day is dangerous.'

'Molly!'

Her mother was beckoning. So she dropped a pound coin into the man's long hand.

His fingers closed over it and he smiled. 'Remember,' he said. 'Wear it only six times. Not once more! And keep it safe. I have an enemy who would like to steal it.'

At home, Molly's mother sewed and ironed the dress. She looked at it doubtfully.
'I'm surprised you like this. It's a bit old-fashioned. When will you wear it?'
Molly took the dress and held it against herself. 'Can I wear it to the beach tomorrow?'
'Only if it's sunny,' her mother said.

Next morning the sky was still and pale, as if it hadn't made up its mind what to do.

'Please be sunny!' Molly whispered. She crossed to the wardrobe and opened it and stared in surprise.

The dress was yellow.

Yellow as a cornfield, or a beach. As she pulled it on, the material had changed; it was heavy and slithered down her arms and against her legs as if the dress was made of sand.

Downstairs, Mum looked over the newspaper. 'Very nice.'

'What about the colour?' Molly asked cautiously.

Her mother shook her head. 'Hard to tell. It's a mixture, isn't it? Like a rainbow.'

Molly looked down at herself. 'It's yellow,' she whispered.

The baby, Daniel, gurgled in his chair. Suddenly Mrs Davies put the paper down.

'It's a lovely day,' she said. 'Let's go to the seaside.'

They went in the car. When they got there, the beach was wide and wet from the tide. The rock pools were full of limpets and charcoal-grey cockles. Molly ran in and out of the waves and buried Danny in the sand and crowned him with necklaces of seaweed and shells like a sea-baby.

That night, in the wardrobe, from the hem of the dress sand grains trickled.

On the second day, Molly said, 'I'd really like it to be hot today.'

She opened the wardrobe door.

The dress was red. She took it out carefully, the soft silk fragile and light as poppy petals.

All day the sun burned in the sky. Mrs Davies hung a piece of awning from a tree and lay in her hammock, sewing.

The garden sizzled with butterflies; everywhere Molly went, they drifted after her, as if the dress scattered pollen or honey.

She sprawled in the shade under the hedge and gazed up through the leaves.

Why did no-one notice the dress change colour? Could she have any weather she wished for?

Next morning, in bed, she wished
for a wind to blow the leaves down.

The dress slid off its hanger and it was brown! Brown as conkers, the hem all cobwebbed.

She raced and twirled down the street. The wind gusted the leaves in an autumn gale, snaking her hair out. At the corner it almost lifted her up, giddy as a leaf.

She swung round the pillar-box.

On the other side of the road, a woman stood looking in the baker's window.

But she wasn't looking at cakes or pastries; she was looking at Molly's reflection, and when she turned, her eyes were dark as night.

She was there that evening too, under the lamppost in the street. Molly dropped the edge of the curtain and jumped into bed, pulling the bedclothes tight.

She knew the woman wanted the dress.

And what would happen if Molly wore it seven times?

Next morning she had to go to the shops. 'I want it to be foggy, so no-one can see me.'

Her mother counted money into her hand. 'Don't take too long, and be careful crossing the road.'

Outside, Molly looked round. No-one was there. She ran all the way to the shops, the sky above her misty and damp.

Coming out, she stopped in fright.

The woman was waiting on the pavement. 'Hello, Molly,' she said.

Molly walked faster.

'My name is Luna,' the woman whispered. 'I'd really like that dress of yours. Look, I've got this one you can have instead.' She showed a handful of white silk, rich with ribbons and pearls. 'A princess's dress.'

'I like mine,' Molly muttered.

The woman caught hold of her; her nails were long and sharp. 'But I've got you now,' she hissed.

At once the fog came down.

It drifted over houses and cars, over the hedges. Molly tugged herself free and raced into it, deep in the cold misty droplets.

She ran through crystals and clouds. Noises were muffled; she bumped into walls, and had to feel her way along the hedge.

All the time Luna was close behind, calling, 'Molly! Come back!'

Molly's fingers touched a cold iron gate. She was home! She ran up the path, slamming the front door tight behind her.

Her mother came out of the kitchen. 'What a fog! I thought you'd get lost.'

ext day Molly wished for rain. She stayed in and wore jeans.
But when the clock struck seven, the dress turned blue.

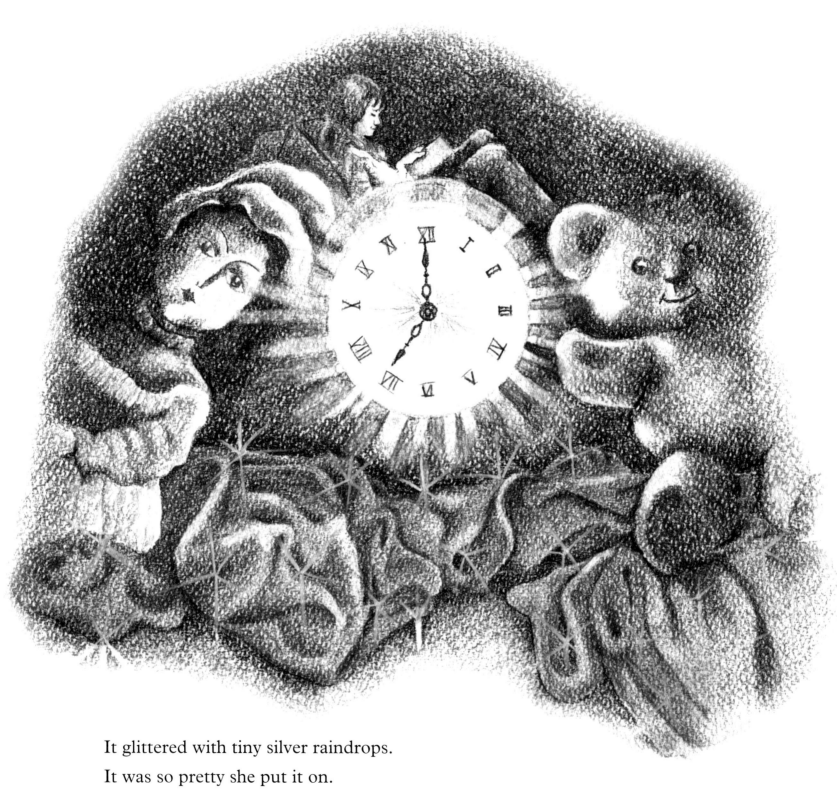

It glittered with tiny silver raindrops.
It was so pretty she put it on.

In the garden, soft rain was falling. She crept out past the sleeping cat. Carefully, she unbolted the door.

Luna didn't look ordinary now.

She was tall, her eyes sharp and hungry. There were animals all around her, snakes and cats, the dark slither of a wolf.

'This is my dress,' Molly said, stubborn.

'Listen to me.' Luna smiled. 'That dress is made of time and air. You can only wear it once more. Why not sell it to me! I could give you anything you want.'

22

Molly thought.

She thought of toys and holidays, of puppies and a big house.

She thought about being clever, and everyone liking her at school.

Then she shook her head.

'Are you sure?' Luna whispered.

Molly stepped back. 'Tomorrow I'll wear it for the last time.
Then I'll decide.'

Next morning Molly made her wish.
Her room was lit with a strange glow.
She rubbed frost off the window
and stared with delight.

The garden was white with snow.
The dress, crumpled on the chair, was
white too, with ermine fur around the collar
and wrists.

But all day, as she built a
snowman for Danny, she shivered
and couldn't keep warm. Was the
dress annoyed with her?

'That old thing is no use,'
her mother said at last. 'I'm
sending it to a charity shop.
Take it off and put something
else on.'

So she did. At once the snow began to melt. By teatime only a few crusted heaps
were left.

Danny cried and had to be put to bed.

After tea Molly was worried. It grew dark early and the street was quiet. She went and looked at the dress, then picked it up and ran down to the garden.

'Where are you?' she whispered.

'Here. Down here.'

The end of the garden was a shadow of trees. Luna was waiting.
She held her hands out eagerly.

'No.' Molly hugged the dress tight. 'I've decided to keep it.'

'But you can't wear it for a seventh time.'

'I can.'

'You wouldn't dare,' Luna said.

Molly felt stubborn. 'Just watch me.' She stepped into the dress, pulled it on over her clothes and buttoned it.

'There,' she said.

Luna laughed. She spread her arms and her hair blew in the sudden gale. The trees thrashed and crackled.

The wolves howled.

'At last!' she cried. 'Your power is ended! Now the weather will obey *me*!'

Molly looked down.

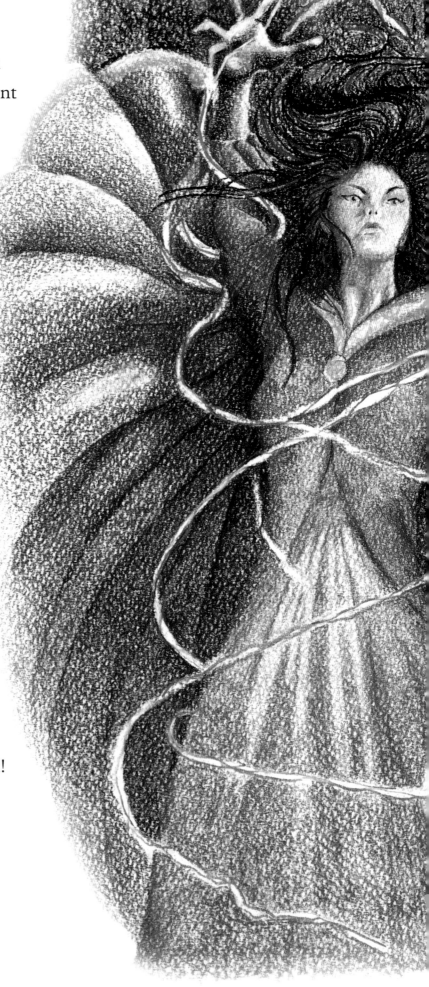

The dress had turned

black.

The sky was black too.

Lightning flickered; thunder rumbled with a great roar.

Twigs flew past Molly's face. Rain stung the last leaves in a downpour.

'Give it to me!' Luna hissed. 'And I'll stop the storm!'

Molly's hair was in her eyes. Rain made the buttons slippery; she tugged at them.

'Hurry!' Luna cried.

Molly stepped out of the dress.

At once Luna grabbed.

'It's mine!'

'No!' Molly held on tight. The storm was raging and the rain streamed down.

They pulled the dress between them. It tore like a flash of lighting.

'I've got it!' Luna cried.

But another hand snatched the dress away.

'No you haven't,' Sol said. He was standing under the trees.

As soon as she saw him, the woman hissed and backed into darkness. 'One day,' she whispered, 'that dress will be mine.' Then she faded like smoke.

Sol folded the dress, smoothing it, calming it. Molly realised the rain had stopped. Water dripped from the branches onto her hair.

'I'm sorry,' she whispered.

Sol smiled and turned towards the house. 'You should be. It was wrong to wear the dress again. But you saved it from her. It was lucky I came in time.'

'Who is Luna?'

Sol looked back at the trees. 'My shadow. Night and darkness. But you won't have to worry about her again.'

In the black sky the stars were coming out, one by one.

Molly touched the dress. 'Did the dress change the weather or the weather change the dress?'

The thin man smiled. 'Who knows? Perhaps it was you changing them both. Goodbye, Molly,' he said. 'The dress must find its new owner now. But I'm sure we'll meet again.'

She stood with her hand on the gate and waved.

'I hope so,' she said softly.